First published in English copyright © 1998 Abbeville Press.
First published in French copyright © 1997 Editions Nathan, Paris. All rights reserved
under international copyright conventions. No part of this book may be reproduced or
utilized in any form or by any means, electronic or mechanical, including photocopying,
recording, or by any information storage and retrieval system, without permission in
writing from the publisher. Inquiries should be addressed to Abbeville Publishing Group,
22 Cortlandt Street, New York, NY 10007. The text of this book was set in Journal Text.
Printed and bound in France.

First edition
2 4 6 8 10 9 7 5 3 1

Library of Congress Cataloging-in-Publication Data
Floury, Marie-France.
Puss in Boots : a fairy tale / by Perrault ; adapted by Marie-France Floury ;
illustrated by Charlotte Roederer.
p. cm. — (The little pebbles)
Summary: A clever cat wins his master a fortune and the hand of a princess.
ISBN 0-7892-0422-3
[1. Fairy tales. 2. Folklore—France.] I. Perrault, Charles. 1628–1703. Chat botté.
II. Roederer, Charlotte, 1967– ill. III. Title. IV. Series.
PZ8.F64Pu 1998
398.2'0944'04529752—dc21   97-23047

Puss in Boots

A Fairy Tale by Perrault

Adapted by Marie-France Floury
Illustrated by Charlotte Roederer

The
Little Pebbles
· Abbeville Kids ·
A Division of Abbeville Publishing Group
New York · London · Paris

Once upon a time there was an old farmer with three sons. When he died, he left the oldest son a windmill, the second son a donkey, and the youngest son a cat.

"What a way to split things up," groaned the youngest son. "My brothers can make flour with the windmill and take it to the market with the donkey. I can eat my cat or make a coat from the fur but after that I have nothing. What can I do?"

The cat understood all of this and began to worry. This cat also could talk, so he spoke to his master.

"Don't cry, master. I am very smart. If you do as I say, everything will work out fine, thanks to me! Just give me a bag and some boots so I can walk through the bushes. I'll amaze you!"

The young man, astonished to hear his cat talk, decided to trust him, and brought him all that he had asked for.

The cat pulled his boots on, slung the bag over his shoulder, and disappeared into the woods.

Soon he came to a clearing, where he picked some wild oats and put them into the bag. Then he lay down and played dead. Before long, a young, not very smart, rabbit hopped into the bag, thinking he would have a feast. Then, quick as a wink, the cat leaped up and closed the bag.

"Ah, a nice little rabbit I can give to the King," said Puss in Boots.

Once at the castle, the cat asked to see His Majesty.

"Sire, I bring you this wild rabbit caught this morning by the Count of Carabas," said the cat in his most respectful voice.

"I do not know the Count," said the King, "but this gives me great pleasure. Please thank him for me."

The cat, of course, had made it all up. The Count of Carabas was the farmer's youngest son. Puss in Boots returned to his master, but said nothing of what had happened.

A few days later, Puss in Boots went hunting once again. In a field of golden wheat, the clever cat hid himself and held his bag wide open. Soon, two partridges flew in, looking for food. Quick as a wink, the cat leaped up and closed the bag.

"Ah, two lovely partridges that I can take to the King," said Puss in Boots.

This time the King saw the cat coming, thanked him, and invited him to have something to drink.

As the months went by, Puss in Boots kept hunting, both to feed his master and to please the King.

One morning, the cat learned that the King would be taking a walk by the river with his daughter.

"Master, the moment has come when I can fulfill my promise to you," said Puss in Boots to the youngest son. "You must do exactly as I say. You must go swimming, and I'll go to the river with you."

"My cat, I do not understand," answered the young man, "but I'll do as you say."

Soon, while the false Count was swimming, the King and his daughter passed by. Then, quick as a wink, Puss in Boots cried, "Help! Help! The Count of Carabas is drowning!"

The King recognized the cat and the name of
the Count who had given him so many gifts.
At once, the King ordered his guards to help the
drowning man.

"Sire," said the cat, "thieves stole my master's
clothes while he was swimming. He cannot show
himself to you without his clothes!" The cat, of
course, had made it all up—he had hidden his
master's clothes himself.

"Give the Count some of my own clothes,"
said the King.

In the King's clothes, the farmer looked very handsome. His Majesty invited the young man to walk with them. The Princess found him so handsome that she fell in love with him.

The cat was thrilled: so far, his plan had worked. He ran on ahead of the King's carriage and spoke to some peasants mowing grass in the fields: "Tell the King that everything here belongs to the Count of Carabas. If you don't, I'll chop you into little bits and bake you in a pie!"

And so when the King asked, "Whose fields are these?" the peasants all answered: "Your Majesty, they belong to our good master, the Count of Carabas."

The cat went on down the road, stopping only to tell all those he found working in the fields: "If the King asks whose hay this is, you must tell him that it belongs to the Count of Carabas. If you don't, I'll chop you all into little bits and bake you in a pie!"

And when the King asked, "Whose hayfields are these?" the frightened peasants all answered: "Your Majesty, all the hay and all the fields belong to our kind master, the Count of Carabas!" The King was very impressed. The clever cat, of course, had made it all up. In truth, all the fields belonged to a frightful ogre.

The cat now went to visit the ogre at his castle. After greeting him politely, the cat said to the ogre, "Sir, I understand that you can change yourself into any animal you wish—I would like to see that!"

"Certainly," said the ogre, and he changed into a lion.

Puss in Boots had to run as fast he could to the roof of the castle. But the lion changed back into the ogre, and so the cat said:

"That's a pretty neat trick. But changing yourself into something smaller—a rat or a mouse—can you do that, too?"

"Of course I can," said the ogre, and he changed himself into a little mouse scurrying across the floor. Then, quick as a wink, Puss in Boots caught the mouse and ate him up—as all cats do with mice.

The cat then ran back up the road to greet the carriage of the King. "Sire, I welcome you to the castle of the Count of Carabas!"

The King was astounded at all the treasures in the castle.

The Princess entered the castle on the arm of the Count. There they found the ogre's feast already served, and what a feast it was!

And what a happy ending this story has, too—the King gladly let his daughter marry the Count, and Puss in Boots became lord of the manor. He no longer chased mice, except for fun.

And so the moral of the story is that even a farmer, if he's nicely dressed, can marry a princess. If he has no wealth, all he needs is a cat.

Look carefully at these pictures from the story.
They're all mixed up. Can you put them back
in the right order?

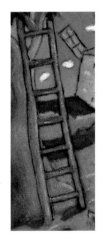